The Go-Away bird sat up in her nest,
With her fine grey wings and her fine grey crest.

A little green bird flew into the tree.
"I'm the Chit-Chat bird. Will you chat with me?
We can talk of the weather, and other things
Like the colour of eggs, and the aches in our wings."
But the Go-Away bird just shook her head
And what do you think she said?

"Go away! Go away! Go away!
I don't want to talk today.
You're much too chatty; you're oh so scatty.
Just the sound of you drives me batty,
So listen to what I say:

Go away!
Go away!
Go away!"

A little red bird flew into the tree.
"I'm the Peck-Peck bird. Will you eat with me?
There are juicy berries on every twig.
We can peck, peck, peck till we both grow big."

But the Go-Away bird just shook her head
And what do you think she said?

"Go away! Go away! Go away!
I don't want to eat today.
Your eyes are beady; you're much too greedy.
Just to look at you makes me seedy,
So listen to what I say:

Go away!
Go away!
Go away!"

A little blue bird flew up to the tree.
"I'm the Flip-Flap bird. Will you fly with me?
We can spread our wings; we can soar up high.
We can cartwheel all through the bright blue sky."

But the Go-Away bird just shook her head
And what do you think she said?

"Go away! Go away! Go away!
I don't want to fly today.
You're whirly and whizzy and much too busy.
Just the sight of you makes me dizzy,
So listen to what I say:

Go away!
Go away!
Go away!"

A brown bird hovered above the tree.
"Good day – I'm the Get-You bird," said he.
"I see I'm in for a special treat.
You're the very bird that I want to eat."

But the Go-Away bird just shook her head
And what do you think she said?

"Go away! Go away! Go away!
I don't want to be your prey.
I'm feeling wary; you're much too scary.
The situation is getting hairy,
So listen to what I say:

Go away!
Go away!
Go away!"

But the Get-You bird said,
"Now that I've met you,

I'm going to
get you,
get you,
get you!"

Then a yellow bird waddled towards the tree.
"Hello – I'm the Come-Back bird," said he.
He opened his bill and began to quack,

"Come back!
Come back!
Come back!
Come back!"

And back flew the others,

one,

two,   three,

All the way back to the tree!

And the five little birds all rose together –
A noisy mob of fluff and feather,
Red, blue, yellow, and green and grey –

And they chased that brown bird far away.

Then the Go-Away bird
hung down her head

And what do you
think she said?

"You can stay! You can stay! You can stay!
I do want some friends today.
Let's start playing – no delaying!
Let's get hopping and hip-hooraying.
Nobody go away!

rattle

rattle

"Something's squeaking!" said Handa.

"That's Grandad," said Akeyo.

"Wheeling his rusty old bike."

"Can you hear slurping?" said Handa.

"Yes." Akeyo yawned.

"Nan's drinking her bedtime milk."

"Oh no – someone's crying!" said Handa.

"Only my … baby sister,"

said Akeyo, falling asleep.

Thud!

"What's that?" Handa held her breath.

"Maybe it's … a door slamming."

She closed her eyes. "Night night, Akeyo."

thud!

Next morning, Handa woke to a *tap-tap-tapping*.

"Someone's at the door," said Akeyo. "Come in!"

"That's funny," said Handa. "There's no one here."

"Hello!" said Akeyo's mum. "Did you sleep well?"

"Not really," said Akeyo.

"You were all too noisy!"

"We were quiet as mice," said the grown-ups.

"Oh!" said Handa.

"So *who* was making the noise?"

woodpecke

owl

pig

porcupine

pangolin

fox

bush-baby

bat

woodpecker

fox

bat

bush-baby

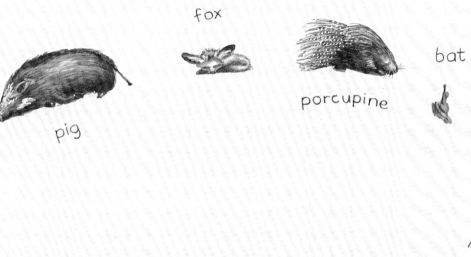

pig

porcupine

pangolin

owl

Discover more Handa titles:

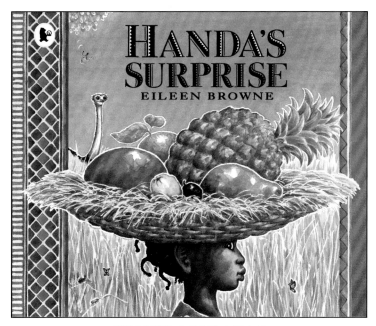

ISBN 978-0-7445-3634-8

ISBN 978-0-7445-9815-5

"So luscious it seems almost edible" *Observer*

"In the best pantomime spirit, readers long
to tell Handa what's happening just
behind her back" *Bookseller*

One of Julia Donaldson's favourite books to share

"This picture book throbs with sunshine.
A stunning book" *Independent*

"Will soon become a firm favourite" *Bookseller*

"A dazzling feast for the eyes that makes
counting fun" *Guardian*

Available from all good booksellers

www.walker.co.uk